THE TORTOISE AND THE HARE

NARRATED BY THE SILLY BUT TRUTHFUL TORTOISE

BY NANCY LOEWEN

ILLUSTRATED BY RUSS COX

Raintree is an imprint of Capstone Global Library Limited, a company incorporated in England and Wales having its registered office at 264 Banbury Road, Oxford, OX2 7DY – Registered company number: 6695582

www.raintree.co.uk
myorders@raintree.co.uk

Edited by Jill Kalz
Designed by Lori Bye
The illustrations in this book were created digitally.
Original illustrations © Capstone Global Library Limited 2019
Production by Kris Wilfahrt
Originated by Capstone Global Library Ltd
Printed and bound in India

ISBN 978 1 4747 6207 6
22 21 20 19 18
10 9 8 7 6 5 4 3 2 1

British Library Cataloguing in Publication Data
A full catalogue record for this book is available from the British Library.

Acknowledgements
Design Element: Shutterstock, Audrey_Kuzman

A fable is a short animal tale that teaches a lesson. It is one of the oldest story forms. "The Tortoise and the Hare" is from a collection of hundreds of fables called *Aesop's Fables*. These stories may have been written by Aesop, a Greek storyteller who lived from 620 to 560 BC.

A hare was teasing a tortoise for being slow.

"Do you *ever* get to where you want to go?" the hare asked, laughing.

"Yes, I do," said the tortoise. "And it doesn't take me *that* long. Let's run a race, and I'll prove it."

The hare thought that was very funny and agreed to the race. The fox set the course and started the runners off.

The hare quickly hopped out of sight. He was so sure he would win the race that he lay down for a nap.

The tortoise walked slowly and steadily. In time he passed the hare, but the hare didn't wake up until the tortoise was near the finish line. Now the hare ran as fast as he could, but he couldn't catch up. The tortoise won!

The moral of the story:

Slow and steady wins the race.

Have you ever seen a tortoise do this?

Or this?

My name is Balderdash, by the way. Funny name, isn't it?
The word *balderdash* means nonsense. Silliness. Rubbish.
But Balderdash is a long name, so just call me Dash.

That little fable you read just now is all true. Those are the
facts. But it left out all the *good stuff* – like how that race
got me started as a comedian! That's right, my job these
days is to make others laugh. Pull up a stump, and I'll tell you
all about it.

Jiffy the Hare was a pain in my neck even before the race. He really *got* on my nerves!

You see, as *hares go*, Jiffy was pretty slow. He couldn't keep up with the other hares! That's why he was always hanging around. Teasing me made him feel more important.

He'd say things like, "Hurry up, glacier!" or "Tag, you're it!" Then he'd bounce around me as if his springs had come unsprung.

Jiffy's teasing helped make me what I am, though. I learned to "look on the funny side". For example, when Jiffy said, "You couldn't even catch a cold," I would make great big slow-motion sneezes. The other animals loved it. Just watch . . .

One day, Jiffy asked me, "Do you ever get *anywhere*?"

"Well, certainly," I replied. "Wherever I go, there I am." And that's when I had my *great* idea. "Hey, let's race!"

Jiffy laughed until his ears jiggled like jelly. "A race!" he said. "You want to race *me*? Have you lost your mind?"

I patted my head. "No, I'm pretty sure it's still here. Come on, let's race!"

Jiffy looked at me, confused.

"What's the matter?" I asked. "Are you scared?"

"Me? Scared of losing a race to *you*?" Jiffy said. "No way!"

Roxy the Fox offered to be the judge. She set up the course. Animals from all over the forest gathered to see the big event: Tortoise versus Hare.

"On your marks . . . get set . . . GO!" said Roxy.

Jiffy was off like a streak.

I was off like a smudge.

But as I moved my short little legs as fast as they would go, all eyes were on me.

I pretended to pant. The animals chuckled. "Hey, what did the snail say when he was riding the tortoise's back?" I called out.

I paused for just the right amount of time.

"WHHEEEEEEE!"

Everyone laughed. I made a funny face, and they laughed harder.

As the animals hooted with laughter, I made a clumsy attempt to tap dance.

There was MORE laughter.

13.

The race went on . . . and on . . . and on.

Every so often, I pretended to trip.

Or I wiped sweat off my face.

14

Or I'd suddenly tuck myself back into my shell, as if I were scared. Then I'd slowly peep my head out.

The crowd loved it.

Do you want to know the best part? Jiffy the Hare was watching me too. I could see him hiding in the bushes. He would watch for a bit, then race ahead. Watch for a bit, then race ahead.

That was a lot of running, even for a hare. The poor thing must have exhausted himself. Near the finish line, there he was – snoring by the side of the path.

I motioned for the crowd to be quiet. I crept closer and closer to the finish line.

When I was just about to cross the line, I let out a loud, super-slow-motion pretend sneeze.

"Ah . . . AH . . . AAAHHH . . . TCHOOOOOOO!"

That woke Jiffy up!

"**What? NOOOO!**" he yelled. He sprinted towards the finish line as fast as he could. But it was too late. I'd won!

"**Not fair! NOT FAIR! Not FAIR!**" Jiffy cried.

I tried to shake Jiffy's paw. "Good race," I said. "I've never had so much fun!"

Jiffy pouted and looked around at all the animals. He looked at me.

Then he let out a little giggle.

And a bigger giggle.

Pretty soon he was rolling around, laughing so hard he could barely catch his breath.

Have you ever had an "aha!" moment? When suddenly you understand something that didn't make sense before? Jiffy was having one of those.

As soon as he managed to stop laughing, Jiffy put a paw on my shell. "Sorry I was so mean before," he said. "You were really great out there, Dash."

Ever since that race, Jiffy and I have been friends. We're partners in comedy too. **Coming soon to a forest near you: The Jiffy and Dash Show!**

Yes, slow and steady might win the race. But slow and *funny* will win you the laughs!

THINK ABOUT IT

How is the character of Dash different from the character of the tortoise in the original fable? How is the character of Jiffy different from the hare?

Explain how the story would change if it was told from Jiffy's point of view.

We all use humour in different ways. Describe a time when being funny helped you to solve a problem.

Do you agree with the fable's original moral, "slow and steady wins the race"? Why or why not? Give examples to support your answer.

GLOSSARY

Aesop Greek storyteller (620–560 BC) whose fables teach a lesson

character person, animal or creature in a story

comedian person whose job it is to be funny

confused uncertain about something

fable short animal tale that teaches a lesson

glacier large, slow-moving sheet of ice

moral lesson about what is right and wrong

point of view way of looking at something

versus against; often abbreviated as "vs"

23

READ MORE

Illustrated Stories from Aesop (Usborne Illustrated Story Collections), Susanna Davidson (Usborne Publishing, 2013)

Orchard Aesop's Fables, Michael Morpurgo (Orchard Books, 2014)

Red Riding Hood Meets the Three Bears (Fairy Tale Mix-ups), Charlotte Guillain (Raintree, 2016)

The Robo-battle of Mega Tortoise vs Hazard Hare: A Graphic Novel (Far Out Fables), Stephanie Peters (Raintree, 2017)

WEBSITES

www.bbc.co.uk/programmes/b03g64r9
Listen to some more stories from Aesop's Fables.

www.bbc.co.uk/guides/z24rxfr
Find out more about different types of stories.

LOOK FOR ALL THE BOOKS IN THE SERIES:

 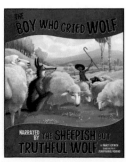 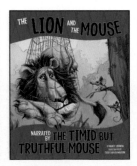 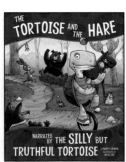